A Total Tip!

by Llinos Mair

Wenfro

O! Gwyn ein byd
– a gwyrdd!

Pont

It was a beautiful summer's day and Mam-gu Iet-wen longed to be outside enjoying the fresh air.

This was just the right weather for a walk, she thought.

Owen and Olwen were outside, playing one of their favourite games. As usual, Olwen went first.

Owen looked very puzzled. Round and round the garden he went, looking for a flower that began with an S.

Who came along but Bwgi-bo, the friendly scarecrow. He had heard voices and laughter and guessed there was a game going on.

Do you need an extra clue, Owen?

Iet-wen

Bwgi-bo smiled. He'd spotted the picture of a snowdrop on the Iet-wen sign but of course, he couldn't speak. Instead, he used little white pebbles to spell out the answer.

3

Before Bwgi-bo had finished his word, Mam-gu Iet-wen came into the garden, singing at the top of her voice. 'Hello little snowdrops, so dainty, so white. La-la la-la…'

It was too late for real snowdrops in the garden now, because it was May. But there was a picture of some on the sign.

Just then, Mam-gu Iet-wen had an idea. 'Who'd like to come for a walk to Dôl-wen meadow to see wild flowers?' she asked.

'Yes, Owen,' replied Mam-gu Iet-wen. But we didn't have a chance to enjoy the wild flowers as we were all too busy celebrating.

On May-day, Gwyn and Gwen, Mam-gu Iet-wen's neighbours, arrange a festival at Dôl-wen meadow. Everyone goes there to welcome the summer.

'I'm going to fetch my crayons,' said Olwen excitedly. She was good at drawing. She had pictures of spring, autumn and winter, and now she wanted to add a summer picture too.

Suddenly, they heard seagulls screeching. 'Oh dear! When seagulls call, rain will fall,' said Mam-gu Iet-wen.

More rain?

Bwgi-bo tweaked his special hat which had a funnel on top. Now, he was all set to catch the water when the rain began to fall.

Mam-gu Iet-wen and the children fetched raincoats and an umbrella, and off they went. As they got closer to Dôl-wen meadow, the screeching of the gulls was deafening.

Oh, what a terrible racket!

Bwgi-bo put his hands over his ears.

Usually, Dôl-wen was a pretty, peaceful place. But something strange had happened.

Bwgi-bo tried his best to block his nose.

The greedy seagulls had torn one bag open and the place was a total tip! Bwgi-bo kept his eyes firmly shut.

I don't want to spy all that with my little eye!

Just then, they heard familiar barking. Pawen, the dog, was running like the wind towards them. The seagulls flew off at once.

Mam-gu Iet-wen saw that there were wild flowers stuck to Pawen's coat. Suddenly a little voice came from somewhere.

Oh dear! Who left this load of rubbish?

Prydwen the spider was sitting on Pawen's back, clinging on to his fur.

'Not Gwyn and Gwen!' said Mam-gu Iet-wen. 'They always leave the place spick and span!'

'They know how important this meadow is for flowers and wildlife,' said Owen.

Suddenly, they heard another screech from the sky. Something was dropping onto their heads.

It was Branwen, the white crow. The Wen-Cam, her special webcam camera back at Iet-wen, had shown her what was happening at Dôl-wen, and she had brought gloves for them all.

'Well done, Branwen,' said Mam-gu Iet-wen as she put on her gloves and passed a pair to Bwgi-bo.

Can I help?

'Yes, you can help, Branwen. Go and ask Gwyn and Gwen to meet us at the meadow as soon as possible,' said Mam-gu Iet-wen. Branwen nodded and off she flew.

'Many hands make light work,' said Mam-gu Iet-wen as she gazed in disbelief at the messy meadow.

'No! There may be all kinds of sharp and dangerous things amongst this dirty rubbish,' said Mam-gu Iet-wen. She wasn't happy for the children to touch a single thing.

Mam-gu Iet-wen carefully untied the first bag. It was light as a feather.

'O dear! We haven't got any recycling bags with us here,' said Mam-gu Iet-wen. Suddenly Bwgi-bo had a bright idea.

He looked up at the sky. There were no clouds to be seen. We won't have rain today, he decided. So he took Mam-gu Iet-wen's umbrella and turned it upside down.

What an excellent idea, Bwgi-bo!

He soon filled the umbrella bin with plastic treasures.

Bwgi-bo moved the small cardboard box that was next to his feet – it made a clinking noise. What do we have here? he thought. Very carefully, he opened the box and found a dozen glass bottles inside.

That's dangerous!

But Bwgi-bo put them to good use. All in a row, they made a good musical instrument.

Just then, they heard a grunting sound.

Peeking over Olwen's shoulder was Rhoswen, the pig, and she was ready to muck in!

Pawen began to sniff at a big blue bucket. Carefully, Rhoswen removed the lid with her nose, and found food!

Bobol bach! A bucketful of vegetable peelings!

Those should be in the Compot!

The Compot was Rhoswen's special compost bin in which she made excellent compost, to help the gardens grow.

In the paper bag they found food cans, plastic and paper, all mixed up. Pawen sung as he worked and used his tail to sort everything into piles.

Swish, swish all the rubbish to keep the meadow clean – and green!

That's a very good tune.

Bwgi-bo jigged as he helped Mam-gu Iet-wen. 'Can I re-use that paper to make a list of all the rubbish?' asked Owen.

21

'Oh, this paper is wet and filthy, Owen. For today, you'll have to ask Olwen for a sheet of clean paper,' said Mam-gu Iet-wen.

Olwen wasn't happy — she wanted to keep the paper to draw pictures of ALL the wild flowers.

Prydwen was busy choosing treasures for the craft box. Bwgi-bo held up some netting that had been used to hold fruit.

Prydwen began to gather all the fruit nets and started to weave them together.

It looks like a giant spider's web!

'We can carry all the treasures back to Iet-wen in this giant net,' explained Prydwen.

Bwgi-bo was inspecting the dirty food cans. Ych a fi! he thought. These would all have to be washed before being recycled — what an unpleasant job. Prydwen had read her friend's mind.

Bwgi-bo smiled. He knew what Prydwen meant.

Bwgi-bo took off the special hat and handed it to Mam-gu Iet-wen.

Bwgi-bo began to twist his bottle-top nose, very carefully. Even though there had been plenty of spring showers lately, he didn't want to waste a single drop of rainwater.

Everyone laughed. Mam-gu Iet-wen managed to catch every drop of water in the big hat and off they went to wash the cans. Drying them would be easy — with the windmill.

Luckily, Gwyn and Gwen arrived just in time to pack everything in the big net. 'Leaving rubbish like this could cause great harm to this wonderful meadow,' said Gwyn.

Gwyn and Gwen thanked everyone for their hard work. 'Next year, we will put up a big sign,' said Gwyn. 'Keep the meadow tidy - take your rubbish home!'

They carried all the treasures back to Iet-wen. Then Olwen had something else to show them - her own special drawing of Dôl-wen, looking clean, peaceful and pretty as a picture.

29

First published in 2016 by Gomer Press, Llandysul, Ceredigion, SA44 4JL
www.gomer.co.uk

ISBN 978 1 84851 862 9
ISBN 978 1 84851 930 5 (ePUB)
ISBN 978 1 84851 942 8 (Kindle)

Part funded by the Welsh Government as part of its Welsh and bilingual teaching and learning resources
commissioning programme.

Ariennir yn Rhannol gan
Lywodraeth Cymru
Part Funded by
Welsh Government

Printed and bound in Wales by Gomer Press, Llandysul, Ceredigion, SA44 4JL